Girls vs. Boys

adapted by Jane Mason and Sarah Hines Stephens

based on "Election" written by Eric Friedman
and "Girls Will Be Boys" written by Jason Gelles & Mike Haukom

Based on *Zoey 101* created by Dan Schneider

SCHOLASTIC INC.

New York   Toronto   London   Auckland   Sydney
Mexico City   New Delhi   Hong Kong   Buenos Aires

ISBN-13: 978-0-439-88258-3
ISBN-10: 0-439-88258-3

Published by Scholastic Inc.
SCHOLASTIC and associated logos are trademarks and/or registered trademarks of Scholastic Inc.

12 11 10 9 8 7 6 5 4 3 2 1   7 8 9 10 11/0

Printed in the U.S.A.
First printing, January 2007

Running for President

Zoey Brooks took a deep breath of the salty ocean-scented air and felt the California sea breeze in her shoulder-length blond hair. It was another beautiful morning on the Pacific Coast Academy campus. Dressed in her new black skirt and long-sleeve boatneck sweater with sporty green, white, and yellow stripes down the sleeves, contrasting orange neck and cuffs, and a colorful tie belt, Zoey Brooks was ready for whatever the day had in store — except for one thing. Her caffeine levels were dangerously low. So she stopped at the new coffee cart on campus to buy herself a large mocha java.

"Hey, Zoey, you coming to class?" her roommate Lola Martinez asked, coming up behind her. She had her black-and-yellow-streaked hair tied off in a neat side ponytail and wore hip plaid gauchos, a burgundy tank, and a white jacket. Chunky, colorful beads circled her neck. No denying, the girl had some funky style.

"Yeah," Zoey said. "Hold on a sec."

"'Kay." Lola smiled and took in the scene, waving at a cute boy from one of her classes. "So, how's the PCA coffee?" she asked, turning back around and eyeing Zoey's cup.

"Awesome!" Zoey replied, giving her drink a final stir and snapping on a lid. She couldn't wait to take a sip. "You should get one."

"Yeah?" Lola asked, raising an eyebrow. That was a pretty solid endorsement. But she wasn't about to spend money on something without trying it out first. Would she buy a new outfit without seeing how it fit? She gracefully lifted the cup out of Zoey's hand and took a sip. "Oooh, that is good." So good she didn't want to let it go. Smiling her thanks, she turned away from Zoey and headed to class.

Zoey stared after Lola, dumbfounded. She had told her roomie to get a coffee drink of her own, not steal hers! "Uh, Lola," she said. Hello? Where was Lola going with *her* cup? Grabbing her oversize army backpack off the cart, Zoey tailed her coffee and her friend. Lola showed no sign of slowing. The girl was unbelievable!

In French class, Zoey and Lola's third roommate,

Nicole Bristow, was already in her seat with her laptop open. "Hey, where ya been?" she asked as Lola came into the room.

"I stopped to buy coffee," Lola replied casually, setting her large shopping-style bag down on the desk in front of Nicole.

"No, she stopped to steal *my* coffee," Zoey corrected, whizzing by and snatching her cup out of Lola's unsuspecting hand and giving the thief a look.

Nicole looked from one roommate to the other, then back at her computer. Good time to change the subject. "Oooh, guys, check out my horoscope," she said excitedly. "'All stars point to romance. That special someone you've been hoping to meet is closer than you *think*.'" She emphasized the last word and sat back in her chair, twirling a lock of her long, straight, brown hair. She wondered if she'd dressed appropriately for the impending romance — was her periwinkle-and-pink-striped tee with the puffy sleeves special enough for her special someone?

"Ooooh, maybe it's him," she said, pointing with her chin at a boy sitting off to the left in the front row. "Do you think it's him?"

The boy looked over in Nicole's direction and smiled. "Hey, how ya doing?" he said.

Nicole sat up straighter. He was cute!

But a second later another girl sat down next to the boy and gave him a hug.

"I'm thinking it's not him," Lola answered, rolling her eyes. Nicole could be so silly.

Zoey peered closer at Nicole's computer screen. Something was off. "This is the horoscope for Capricorn," she said, confused. "You're not a Capricorn."

Nicole eyed her best friend sheepishly. "I know, but I like this one better than mine," she admitted. What was the big deal? She was just being creative. . . . She had to do something to keep herself from falling asleep before class started. "Oooh." She eyed Zoey's coffee cup. "Gimme," she said, snatching it from her friend just as Chase strolled into the room, his dark curls bobbing.

"Whassup, people?" Chase waved at his friends.

"Hi."

"Hey, Chase."

"Morning."

"Hey, did you guys finish the homework last night? 'Cause I got up to chapter seven and totally fell —"

"Hello, Chathe!" a perky voice interrupted. Chase turned around and found himself face-to-face with a girl named Melissa. Lately she'd been kind of . . . everywhere.

4

"Um, oh, hi, Melissa," Chase said awkwardly. He didn't want to be rude, but the girl was practically standing on top of him.

"Chathe," Melissa scolded, batting her eyelashes and lisping. "Don't call me Melitha. Melitha thoundth tho theriouth. Call me Mel."

"All right, Mel . . ." Chase said awkwardly.

"I thaved you a theat!" Melissa squealed, dragging Chase over to a seat across the aisle.

Chase took off his backpack and adjusted his dark red long-sleeve surf shirt. "All right, I guess I'll be sitting here," he grumbled. Not the seat he would have chosen, for sure. But at least class only lasted an hour. . . .

"Mmmmm, how great is this coffee?" Nicole said, taking another sip from Zoey's cup and fiddling with the little cardboard jacket that kept the hot drink from burning her fingers.

"I wish I knew," Zoey grumbled. She hadn't had a single sip!

Chase drummed his fingers on the desk and tried to ignore the intense way Melissa was staring at him. It wasn't easy.

"Bonjour, étudiants," their French teacher greeted the kids as she came into the room. "Before we get started I've been asked to read this announcement." She strolled up the center aisle and turned to face her class.

"Elections for ninth-grade class president will be held next Friday. Students who wish to run must be nominated no later than —"

"I nominate Zoey!" Chase called out, shooting his hand into the air.

"Yeah!"

"She's perfect!"

"Great idea!"

Several other kids voiced their support of Chase's suggestion.

"Huh?" Zoey looked totally surprised. She had zero interest in running.

"I second Zoey's nomination!" Nicole crowed.

Zoey shot her roommate a look. Did anyone even think of asking her what she thought? "Hold on a second," she said, but not loudly enough.

"All right, Zoey Brooks is officially on the ballot," the teacher announced.

Zoey turned to Chase — the person who started all of this. "Chase!" she protested.

"Sorry, Zo'," he said with a shrug. "You're on the ballot. That means you gotta run."

Zoey narrowed her eyes at her best guy friend, then got an idea. "Fine," she said, raising her hand and addressing the teacher. "I nominate Chase."

The teacher wrote Chase's name on the ballot next to Zoey's.

"Wait, uh, hold up a minute," Chase said. Now things were starting to get out of hand.

"Does anyone second the nomination for Chase?" the teacher called, looking around the room.

Chase shook his head. "No," he piped up. "No one does."

Next to him, Melissa's hand shot up like a rocket. "I abtholutely thecond the nomination for Chathe," she said excitedly.

"Melissa!" Chase protested.

"Any more nominations?" the teacher asked. "No? *Très bien*. I'll just take these names to Mr. McClure and be back in a sec." The teacher smiled at her students before walking back down the aisle and out the door.

As soon as she was out of earshot Zoey turned to Chase. "I don't want to be class president!" she protested.

"I don't, either," Chase agreed.

"Ooooh, Zoey, check out your horoscope," Nicole said, consulting her screen. "You will win a major competition," she read. "Is that freaky or what?" she added in an excited whisper.

Zoey squinted at the computer. "That's for Virgo. I'm not a Virgo," she said.

"Shhhh!" Nicole shushed her. "Don't tell people."

"Oh, oh!" Melissa said from across the aisle. "Can you read my horothcope? I'm a Thagittariuth." She smiled at Chase, leaning close to him and squeezing his arm. "I'm a Thagittariuth," she repeated.

Chase tried to ignore the gross feeling of Melissa's saliva splattering on his face. The girl was a spitter. "Of course you are," Chase said, wiping his cheek. French class could not be over soon enough.

CHAPTER 2

Friendly Pact

Chase followed Zoey out of the Language Arts building. "Why'd you nominate me?" he asked, coming up alongside her.

"'Cause you nominated me," Zoey replied easily.

"Well, I happen to think that you'd make a great choice for class president," Chase explained as they headed up a flight of outdoor stairs.

"Okay, and I think you would." Zoey looked at him from behind her long blond bangs.

"Well . . . thanks, but I don't want to run against you."

"Ooooh, what's the matter? You afraid you're gonna lose?" Zoey could not resist the chance to tease Chase. It was so easy to get him riled, and he was funny when he was mad.

"No, I'm not afraid I'm gonna lose," Chase said, though he hadn't actually given winning or losing much thought. He just had a feeling that running against Zoey was a bad idea.

"Oooh. So you think you can beat me?" Zoey asked, pretending to be offended.

"No, no!" Chase said worriedly. How could he explain without making things worse? "I mean, I don't think I could beat you," he mumbled.

Zoey smiled. Chase was getting too worked up. She decided to let him off the hook a little. "Calm down. I'm just playing with you."

"Look, I'm just worried," Chase admitted. "'Cause, you know, we're really good friends, and I'm afraid that if we're running against each other, you know, the competition will screw up our friendship." There — he'd been honest — was that so hard?

Zoey stopped and turned toward Chase. "Okay, then let's make a pact," she suggested.

Chase raised an eyebrow. This could be interesting. "What kind of pact?"

"That no matter what happens in this election we both promise not to let it affect our friendship," Zoey said, making it sound like a piece of cake.

That sounded great. "Deal," Chase said. He spit onto his right palm. "Spit shake."

Zoey made a face. "Ew, gross." She eyed Chase's hand like it was covered in something way more offensive than spit.

Chase looked a little embarrassed. "What, girls don't spit shake?"

"Not really," Zoey confirmed. Like anyone would want to.

"Well, hello!" somebody interrupted.

Chase waved at the PCA teacher with the booming voice, continental accent, and great timing. "Oh, hey, Mr. Edwards," he called.

"I've just heard that you two will be running for class president," Mr. Edwards said proudly. He held out a hand to Zoey. "Zoey, good luck," he said, giving her hand a firm shake.

"Thanks."

"Chase!"

"Oh, you don't want to . . ."

Mr. Edwards grabbed Chase's hand before he could warn him. No sooner were their hands clasped together than Mr. Edwards made a disgusted face.

Chase winced. He just spit shook a teacher! "Oh, that's just —"

"I don't want to know," Mr. Edwards insisted, wiping his hand on his blue shirt and walking away looking totally grossed out.

Chase and Zoey chuckled as they watched him go. Nasty!

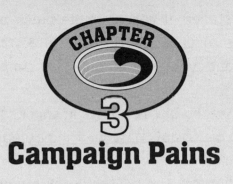

Campaign Pains

Across campus in the girls' lounge, Zoey, Lola, and Nicole were working hard on Zoey's campaign posters.

"Okay, Zo', check this out!" Nicole held up a large purple-and-orange poster with a cute picture of Zoey in the middle and glittery writing all around it. "'Yo-yo yo-ey, vote for Zoey,'" she read, shrugging her shoulders in excitement.

Zoey shot her roommate a "you've got to be kidding" look. Nicole was a great friend, but sometimes you had to wonder what was rattling around behind her big brown eyes.

Nicole got a read on Zoey's look and pushed out her lower lip in a pout. "What, it's my fault nothing good rhymes with your name?" she protested.

"Okay, what do you guys think of this?" Lola interrupted, holding up her own poster.

Zoey stared. It was a simple black poster with a giant picture of Chase . . . dressed in a strapless wedding gown and veil! The slogan was simple: SAY NO TO CHASE!

Zoey stared at the poster in shock. "Okay, where did you get a picture of Chase wearing a wedding dress?" she had to ask.

Lola giggled. The poster definitely made a statement. "I didn't. I took his head and photo-doc'ed it onto some girl's body."

Zoey still didn't get it. "Uh, why?"

"Because if you want to win this election you need to set yourself apart from the other candidates. And the best way to do that is to make people think your opponent is a weirdo." It was all so simple — and easy to manipulate!

"Thanks, but I don't want to win that way," Zoey said. She wanted to run a fair race. If the majority of students wanted Chase to be their president, then so be it. She'd never even wanted to run for class president, anyway.

"Hello, peers!" a high-pitched voice came out of nowhere, greeting the girls. Quinn Pensky, PCA's smartest student, stood behind the couch dressed in a purple PCA tee and funky paisley skirt.

"Hey, Quinn," the girls replied.

"Wanna help us make some posters?" Nicole asked.

Quinn shook her head hard enough to make the feathers tied to the ends of the braids that framed her face flutter wildly. "Sorry, I can't," she said, eyeing them from behind her square-framed glasses.

"Why not?" Nicole asked. It wasn't like they'd asked her to write speeches or take polls.

"'Cause," Quinn practically shouted, pulling a campaign poster out from behind her back. It read: VOTE MARK DEL FIGGALO! HE'LL MAKE THINGS BETTER. In the center of the poster was a giant photo of Quinn's beefy boyfriend, Mark, squinting into the camera. He looked miserable — almost like he was in pain. "My future husband has entered the race!" Quinn squealed.

"Who's he?" Lola asked bluntly, shaking her head at the pathetic picture.

"Mark Del Figgalo," Quinn replied proudly. "Is this the face of a born leader or what?" she asked, grandly pointing to the picture.

Nicole tried to smile supportively. "What," she murmured quietly, hiding her smile behind a hand.

The door to the lounge opened. "In here, Mark!" Quinn crowed as the same chunky guy from the photo ambled into the room holding a handful of campaign buttons.

"Vote for me, I'll make things better," he told Zoey in a monotone, handing her a button.

Lola was next. "Vote for me, I'll make things better," he vowed woodenly.

Nicole was the final lucky recipient of a button. "Vote for me, I'll make things better," Mark repeated with the gusto of an automaton.

The girls stared at the buttons. They all featured the same horrible picture of Mark and bland slogan.

"You can't buy that kind of charisma!" Quinn cooed, running after her boyfriend gleefully.

Nicole squinted at her button. "Mark is running?" she asked in disbelief.

"Mark's last name is Del Figgalo?" Zoey added.

In an instant Quinn reappeared. "It means 'of the figs,'" she explained importantly before chasing her beau back out the door. There was campaign work to do!

Across campus in the guys' room, Chase's roommate and best boy bud, Michael Barrett, was helping Chase make some campaign posters of his own. Michael thought it was great that his roommate was running for president and was more than happy to help out. He was just finishing up a poster when the guys' third room-mate, Logan Reese, sauntered into the room and slapped Chase a low five.

"Whassup, future prez?" he asked, looking casual in his black tank with a tiny skull printed near the heart, a beaded necklace, and baggy shorts. "Dude, it is going to be so cool when you win the election," Logan proclaimed, tossing the football he was carrying in the air.

Chase looked up at his egomaniac of a roommate. He liked Logan but knew you couldn't really trust the guy. "How's that?" he asked suspiciously.

"'Cause being president equals power, and power attracts girls." Logan raised his eyebrows and nodded knowingly.

"And if Zoey wins?" Chase prompted.

"Ain't gonna happen," Logan replied easily, still tossing the football.

Michael looked up from his poster. "And what makes you so sure?" he inquired.

"Dude . . . she's a girl," Logan said, punching Michael on the arm to wake him up. Duh!

"So?" Chase asked.

"So, PCA's always had guy presidents," Logan explained, since these guys were clearly not picking up on the obvious. "And that's not gonna change if I can help it." He thrust the football into Michael's arms and slid onto the couch between the two dudes.

"What does that mean?" Chase asked.

"It means, I'm going to do whatever it takes to crush Zoey in this election." Logan put his hand on Chase's shoulder for emphasis.

Chase pushed Logan's hand away. "Okay, first of all, I don't want to 'crush' Zoey," he said, making invisible quotation marks in the air with his fingers. "I'm not even sure if I want to win. So don't help me, all right?"

"Okay, chill," Logan said, half eyeing Michael, who was pretending to be a quarterback looking for an open teammate in the end zone. "If you don't want my help, I won't help," he promised, snatching the ball from Michael before he could complete his imaginary play.

"Good," Chase said. But he could not ignore the smirk on Logan's face. . . .

Smoothie Insanity

Nicole sat with both her roommates at one of the outside tables overlooking the Pacific. They'd just finished lunch, and Nicole was in the middle of a giant debate . . . with herself. She stared at the piece of luscious chocolate cake in front of her, clinking her fork on the edge of the plate nervously.

Finally, heaving a giant sigh, she pushed the plate away. "Okay, I shouldn't eat this chocolate cake," she proclaimed.

Lola looked over at the perfectly frosted, perfectly decadent-looking dessert sitting in front of Nicole. "Then why did you take it?" she asked.

"Because I'm weak!" Nicole wailed. Even her turquoise tank with sequins and matching beaded necklace wasn't helping her get through this, and it *always* cheered her up. Why hadn't she been able to resist the cake when she saw it in the dessert buffet?

"Here, Zoey, you have it." Nicole pushed the cake toward her friend.

Zoey waved a hand and searched for her self-control. The cake did look delicious, and she wasn't exactly a calorie-counter. But she had been eating a lot of sweets lately. "No, I'm trying to be good." She pushed the plate toward Lola. Then quickly wiped her hand on the Indian-print tank she was wearing over a deep rust silk-screened cap-sleeve T-shirt, as if the chocolate might have seeped onto her fingers. "Lola, you go for it."

"Uh-uh," Lola replied, shaking her head and the backward pink newsboy cap that crowned it. "There's, like, a billion calories in that thing." She made a face and pushed the plate back to where it had started, in front of Nicole.

"All right," Nicole said, suddenly getting an idea. "Here's the plan — we all just eat one bite. Okay?"

Zoey smiled and reached for her fork. Now *that* was a good plan. "Okay," she agreed.

"Just one," Lola agreed, ready to get her fork into that chocolaty sweetness. She could not dive in fast enough!

All three girls stabbed up a bite of cake at the

same time and popped it into their mouths. "Mmmmmmmm," they murmured, chewing contentedly. The cake really was as good as it looked.

"Okay, one more," Zoey suggested after she had savored every single morsel of her single morsel. It was a lot more fun to share decadence with your friends, right? Plus, you didn't have to feel guilty.

"Just one," Lola repeated.

"Mmmmmmm," came the chorus a few seconds later. Zoey was remembering something she'd heard about the therapeutic benefits of chocolate. Wasn't it a cure for depression? It was good for you, right? It sure tasted like it should be.

Zoey was licking chocolaty goodness from the corners of her mouth when Quinn came up to their table. She was dressed in a wild-looking purple-and-blue tie-dye shirt, but in spite of her cheery color palette, the usually perky scientist looked totally down.

"What's wrong?" Zoey asked as Quinn slumped into the seat next to Lola and plunked down the laptop she was carrying.

"I've been collecting polling data for the election," Quinn told them as she opened her computer.

"Really?" Nicole asked.

Zoey was intrigued. "So . . . how'm I doing?"

"You're doing fine," Quinn half mumbled, giving Zoey a sad sideways glance. She hit a few buttons on her keyboard. "Here, I'll show you." She turned the computer toward the other girls so they could see for themselves.

The screen showed a graph with colored bars representing each of the candidates.

"See, Zoey, you're the blue bar, and Chase is the red bar," Quinn explained.

"Wow, so we're, like, almost tied," Zoey said. She sat up straighter and the large beaded hoops that dangled from her ears bobbed with excitement. Their bars were basically the same height — she and Chase were both doing great!

"Yup," Quinn said dejectedly. "You each have about forty-nine percent of the vote."

Nicole leaned in closer, squinting at the screen. "What's that tiny little green line down there?" she asked.

Quinn sighed. "That's Mark's bar. He's not doing so well," she admitted, shaking her head sadly. "My poor, sweet baby. How can people not be voting for him?" She gestured dramatically toward one of Mark's campaign posters set up on a stand behind them — the one with the terrible squinty photo. "Look at that face!"

The other three girls exchanged glances. "I don't know," Nicole said. She would rather *not* look at that face. . . .

"It's really weird," Lola agreed, giving Quinn a sympathetic look. It must have been hard to live in a completely different universe.

Just then Melissa and a couple of other ninth-grade girls raced up to their table. "Hey, you guyth!" Melissa squealed. "If you go down to the quad you can get a free thmoothie. And look! Chathe'th fathe ith on the thide of the cup!" She pointed at the decal with Chase's smiling mug before slurping another sip of the smoothie through her straw. She was so excited, her hands were practically shaking.

Chase smoothies? Zoey eyed the cup warily. Something was up — something fishy. She and her friends were on their feet in an instant, heading down to the quad to see for themselves.

But before Zoey could see anything, she could hear. And what she heard made her roll her eyes.

"That's right, PCA students, free smoothies!" Logan's voice boomed through a megaphone. ". . . Compliments of Chase Matthews. Remember . . . a vote for Chase is a vote for free smoothies!"

Behind Logan, hoards of PCA students were

grabbing for the paper cups with Chase's picture on the front.

Zoey advised herself to keep cool as she approached the large smoothie stand. It wasn't easy — especially when she saw Logan's smug face.

"Hey, Zoey," he greeted. "You voting for Chase?" He pointed to the Chase button that was pinned to his PCA T-shirt.

"What are you doing?" Zoey asked, ignoring the question and giving Logan a steely look.

"Just getting out the message." Logan shrugged. Then he raised the megaphone to his lips again. "Vote for Chase!" he called, working the crowd.

A bunch of PCA students cheered in reply.

Nicole stared at the crazy scene. She hated to admit it, but it looked as though Logan's scheme was working. Only where was . . .

"Hey." Nicole tapped Zoey on the shoulder and pointed toward Chase. He was approaching the quad with Michael hot on his heels.

In less than five seconds Zoey was standing in front of the other candidate. "This is how you plan to win the election, by giving away free smoothies?" she demanded.

"I just heard about this," Chase shot back defensively.

"He just heard," Michael echoed, nervously backing him up. An angry Zoey was a force to be reckoned with.

"Well, I don't think it's very fair," Zoey said, planting her hands on her hips.

"Neither do I," Chase agreed. "Which is why I'm going to go put a stop to this right now." He waggled a finger in the direction of the smoothie stand and marched off.

Zoey watched him go, then gave Michael a glare all his own.

"Uh . . . I'm gonna f-follow him," Michael mumbled nervously.

"Uh-huh," Zoey said, her hands still planted firmly on her hips. She watched the back of Michael's kelly-green polo as he hurried to catch up. She couldn't believe that Chase was letting Logan manipulate the race in his favor like this. It was practically out-and-out cheating!

"Hey, here's Chase!" Logan called through the megaphone.

"Whooo, whooo!" the smoothie-drinkers cheered.

Ignoring the crowd, Chase dragged Logan away. "What're you doing?" he asked, furious. This was *not* the way he wanted to run his campaign.

"Helping you get votes," Logan replied, pointing to the life-size standee of Chase next to the smoothie cart. Sheesh. The plan was brilliant and he had financed it himself — or at least his dad had. Couldn't the dude be grateful?

"You said you weren't gonna help me." Chase glared.

"I know — I lied."

"You lied?" Chase asked, flabbergasted. This was a new low — even for Logan.

"Welcome to politics, my friend." Logan punched Chase on the arm before reaching up and grabbing a smoothie from the cart. "Here, have a smoothie."

Chase batted the frozen concoction away. "I don't want a smoothie," he insisted.

"It's mango," Logan taunted in singsong, wagging the cup in front of his friend.

"Ooooh! Mango!" Michael exclaimed. He snatched the cup from Logan's hand without a second thought. Mango was his hands-down favorite flavor.

"Gimme that!" Chase grabbed the cup from Michael before he could take a sip. But once he had it he wasn't sure what to do with it. Thinking fast, he handed it off to a passing student. "Here!"

Scowling at Logan, Chase turned away. The situation was out of hand. He had to talk to Zoey — to try and explain. He had nothing to do with any of this!

Zoey was waiting right where he'd left her, and she didn't look any happier. "Listen, Zoey, I promise I'll make Logan stop the whole free-smoothie thing," he vowed.

"Whatever." Zoey shrugged, still fuming inside. How could Chase let this happen?

Chase had to convince her. This wasn't his fault! "Listen, I really had nothing to do with this. I —"

"Okay, people!" Logan's voice boomed. He was standing on a bench talking to the large crowd that had gathered. "Whaddya get with Chase Matthews?"

"Free smoothies!" the crowd cheered.

"And what do you get with Zoey?"

"Nothing . . . nothing at all!"

Zoey stared daggers at Chase.

"Right. So who do you want for class president?" Logan bellowed.

"Chase! Chase! Chase! Chase! Chase!" the crowd chanted in unison, holding up their cups.

Zoey's glare bored into Chase as he stood there

with his hands in his pockets. He felt like a slimeball. Finally he turned to her.

"Uh, remember how we said we wouldn't let this whole election thing, you know, affect our friendship? Remember that?" he asked, praying that the pact was still in effect.

"Yeah, I remember that," Zoey said, shooting Chase one more disgusted look before turning on her heel and walking away.

"All right," Chase called after her. "I just wanted to make sure that we were cool. I'll call ya later!" he shouted over the chanting smoothie-wielders.

Zoey gave him a "whatever" wave but kept on walking.

This was not good. Worse than Chase could have imagined. "And she hates me," he muttered to himself. At the moment, he could hardly blame her. He wasn't feeling so crazy about himself, either.

President for Sale

"Zoey hates me!" Chase paced in his dorm. Logan's little smoothie giveaway was ruining his relationship with one of his best friends. But did Logan care? No. He was lounging on the sofa, working a handheld video game like nothing was wrong.

"Who cares?" Logan didn't bother to hide his disgust. Chase was ruining his concentration. Couldn't he see he was trying to play? As far as he was concerned, his smoothie plan had gone, well, smoothly. Chase was the name on everyone's lips and the smile on their cups campuswide. "What about your little pact?" he asked. That was supposed to keep Chase in Zoey's good graces, wasn't it? Logan wasn't sure how all that lovey-dovey friendship stuff worked. And he didn't care.

Chase ran a hand through his unruly hair and looked at Michael for a little support.

"Yeah, man, you said Zoey told you no matter what happened in the election she'd be cool with it," Michael reminded Chase. "I thought you spit shook."

"Wouldn't it be spit shaked?"

"It doesn't matter," Chase sighed. They hadn't shaken. "Girls think spit's gross." And even if they had swapped palm spit, what mattered was that Zoey was mad. "The point is that this stupid election is going to wreck my relationship with Zoey," Chase said, feeling helpless and exasperated.

"But she said it wouldn't," Michael argued. Chase needed to relax.

Chase gave Michael a look of utter disbelief. "Were you just born?" he asked. Chase could not believe his friend was so dense. "Don't you know girls don't mean half the stuff they say? Remember that girl you dated a couple of years ago?"

"Oh, yeah." Michael's eyes got big as the memory flooded back. He looked at the computer that was open on his lap and tried to forget, but couldn't. "The Karen Franklin incident," he said softly.

The horror in Michael's voice got Logan's attention. He paused his game. "What happened with Karen Franklin?" he asked.

Michael was happy to tell the story. "Her birthday was coming up, right? So I asked her what she wanted. She said 'nothing,' so I said, 'uh, nothing?' She goes, 'yeah, nothing.' So I said, 'Are you sure?' She's all, 'Yes, I don't want anything.'" Michael shrugged and looked at Chase and Logan. Seemed pretty clear, right? "So I didn't buy her a present."

"And?" Logan asked.

"She cried for three days and moved to Wisconsin." Bye-bye, Karen Franklin. Michael *still* couldn't believe it.

"Wisconsin?" Logan asked. Was he kidding?

"It's the dairy state," Michael said, in case Logan was not familiar with the Midwest.

"Oh." He'd thought Kansas was the dairy state. But wait. "What was the point of this story?" he asked.

"That you need to stay out of my campaign, all right?" Chase let go of the top bunk he had been leaning on and stepped closer to Logan to make sure he was getting this. "I don't want to win in a way that's gonna make Zoey hate my guts."

"All right." Logan turned back to his game. He had no interest in a lecture from Chase Matthews. But Chase wasn't finished.

He pointed an accusing finger at Logan. "I don't

want you buying me any more votes with your evil smoothies! Okay?"

"O-kay," Logan enunciated, rolling his eyes. He got it already.

Chase stared at Logan. The guy had just agreed to stay out of it. But Chase was not so sure — he knew better than to trust Logan.

The next day, there was another frenzy on campus. Somebody was tossing out free money! Students scrambled on the ground and jumped in the air grabbing madly at floating bills. And right in the middle of the money giveaway was Chase. Only the Chase in the melee was made of cardboard. The real guy behind the chaos was holding a megaphone.

"That's right. Vote for Chase. Chase Matthews for class president." Logan put down the megaphone to watch the kids picking money up off the sidewalk and grinned. Cash was even better than smoothies for buying votes. And all Logan had promised was that he would not buy votes with smoothies. . . .

Around the corner, Zoey and Nicole were handing out campaign buttons on their way to class.

"Vote for Zoey!" Nicole called. "Zoey for president!"

Everyone they met seemed to be in such a good mood. Nicole thought maybe they were happy to see her in her new wide-stripe tank top and pink capris. Though she had to admit Zoey's outfit pretty much rocked, too. Nicole especially liked the way the sequin trim on Zoey's short denim skirt coordinated with the sequins on the pink short-sleeve cardigan she wore over her blue print shirt. Neither of them needed a poll to tell them they looked good. Nicole was confident that if fashion counted at all, Zoey was going to win for sure!

"Vote for me!" Zoey called out happily. After yesterday she really wanted to win. Or maybe she just really wanted to beat Chase. "Remember to vote Tuesday," she reminded the people as they passed.

The students were all smiling and taking the buttons. Zoey was beginning to think she might really have a shot at being president . . . until she and Nicole rounded the corner. What she saw made her stomach turn. "Now what?" she wondered aloud.

Two guys in PCA shirts stood on the low concrete retaining wall tossing cash, while below them students grabbed the crisp ones in a frenzy of arms and legs. A voice echoed from the crowd.

"Vote for Chase. Chase Matthews for class

president! When you vote for class president, make sure it's for Chase! Yeah, there's plenty more where this came from."

Zoey didn't have to see who was talking to know who it was. Logan! She pushed her way through the throng and walked straight up to him, with Nicole right behind her. "You're unbelievable!"

Logan just stood there looking smug in his avocado-green muscle shirt. He held a wad of money in his fist. "Well, thank you." It was about time she noticed.

"You're seriously giving people money so they'll vote for Chase?" Zoey demanded.

"Nooo." Logan shook his head. "These are Chase Bucks." Logan held out one of the bills to Zoey, who took it and looked closer.

It felt like a regular dollar. It looked like a regular dollar. But instead of George Washington's face in the center there was a picture of PCA's own Mr. Matthews.

"Okay, what are Chase Bucks?" Zoey wanted to know. This could not be good.

"Chase Bucks can be redeemed for food or merchandise at any store or cafeteria on campus," Logan explained.

"And how's that different from handing out cash?" Zoey asked.

"Simple. Handing out cash is illegal. Handing out Chase Bucks is genius." Logan tapped himself on the chest with his handful of bucks. He was almost too good to be true.

"That's still wrong." Zoey glared.

Nicole, whose mouth had been hanging open in disbelief since they came on the scene, finally found her tongue. "That's just going *around* the rules!"

"How can you do that?" Zoey wondered. How did Logan live with himself?

"You really don't get politics, do you?" Logan asked. He looked at Zoey and Nicole sadly and shook his head. Girls.

Zoey was completely speechless. She was so annoyed, she just had to get away. Heaving a sigh of disgust, she stormed off.

"Hey, where you going?" Nicole called after her friend. She couldn't just leave her here with Logan! Nicole put up her hand to keep the rude dude out of her face and followed Zoey. If this was politics, then she *definitely* didn't get it . . . and she wasn't sure she wanted to.

CHAPTER 6

Locker Room Face-off

Zoey marched into the Stingrays' locker room. Guys in towels scrambled to get out of her way. Not only were they shocked to see a girl in the guys' locker room but she looked seriously peeved.

"Chase!" she called, rounding the bank of lockers. Chase was sitting on a bench, fully dressed in a short-sleeve plaid shirt and jeans. He had a towel draped around his neck and had just finished getting dressed.

When he spotted Zoey he stood up. A guy behind him wrapped in an orange towel spotted Zoey at the same time. He shrieked, clutched his flip-flops to his chest, and ran away.

"What is this?" Zoey demanded, ignoring the panicked guys and holding out a Chase Buck.

"Um, *this* is the guys' locker room." Chase pointed

at the floor before grabbing Zoey's shoulders and looking for a less conspicuous place to stand. "You can't come in here, you're gonna get in trouble."

"*You're* in trouble," Zoey said. Who cared what locker room she was in? She held out the bill again and this time Chase took it.

"Chase Buck," he read. "What is this?"

"They're redeemable at every store on campus," Zoey explained.

"What?" Chase asked, baffled. This was the first he had heard of it.

"Yeah," Zoey confirmed. It was as crazy as it appeared. "Logan's passing out handfuls to every kid in our class so they'll vote for you."

"Man!" Chase was so mad he could just . . . he could . . . SLAM! He pounded the closest metal locker with his bare hand. Mistake. "Ow!" He winced in pain. "Okay, pinky's broken now," he whimpered, hopping around.

"This isn't funny." Zoey tried not to yell, but Chase's clowning was not going to make this problem go away.

"I know. Look, Zoey, you promised me that this election wasn't going to wreck our friendship." Chase's finger was throbbing almost as much as his head. Things were totally spiraling, and it wasn't good.

"Well, I didn't know what kind of campaign you

were going to run," Zoey said in her own defense. Who wouldn't be mad?

"It's not *me!*" Chase insisted. He was stuck between a rock and a Logan place. There was no way out. Or maybe there was. . . .

"All right. Know what? I'm out. I'm done." Chase took his towel off his shoulders and shoved it into his gym bag.

"What do you mean, *done*?" Zoey asked. She hoped he meant he was done buying votes.

"I'm gonna drop out of this stupid race," Chase explained.

Zoey looked at her former friend with disgust. "Oh, so now you're going to *quit* and *let* me win?"

"I didn't say that." Chase was aghast. Zoey was turning this around on him.

"You think the only way I can win is if you drop out." Zoey's head was bobbing. It was all becoming crystal clear.

Chase turned his face skyward and held up his hands. "How is this happening?" he asked the heavens. He could not win for losing!

"You better not quit or I'm gonna be really mad!" Zoey shook a finger at Chase. All she wanted was a fair race.

"Zoey, would you just —" Suddenly Chase had a weird feeling that he was being watched. Turning around, he spotted a crowd of guys in towels who had gathered at the end of the row of lockers. They were listening intently to every word.

When Zoey and Chase looked their way, the guys went back to what they were doing. But the whole scene was so ridiculous. Zoey'd had enough. "I'm out of here," she sighed.

"Zoey!" Chase tried to stop her. He wanted to explain. He wished the whole election would just go away!

Zoey spun around. "Don't you drop out of this election," she repeated.

"Okay" — Chase held up his hands — "I won't drop out."

"Good." Zoey turned to go again.

"So you're not mad at me?" That was all Chase really cared about.

"No. I'm fine," Zoey said. But her tone said something completely different.

"You don't sound fine," Chase pointed out.

"I'm fine," Zoey insisted. "And I can win this election without your help!"

Slander

The next day, sitting at an outside table with her friends, Zoey didn't feel so certain of her victory. They were checking out the latest polls on Zoey's laptop between classes. Chase's red bar was towering above Zoey's blue one. The only person she was beating was Mark. And the showing on his green bar was pathetic.

"There's no way I can win this," Zoey sighed as she snapped the laptop shut. "I'm depressed."

"Oh, come on." Nicole tried to cheer Zoey up. "There are still two days until the election. You could win."

Lola nodded in agreement. Her eyes were wide and her close-fitting teal sequin hat made them shine.

"What makes you say that?" Zoey asked hopefully. Maybe Nicole had some secret polling information or a better source or . . .

"I don't know." Nicole shrugged. "I'm upbeat!"

Zoey smirked. Nicole was the perkiest person she knew. But she was hoping for a better reason.

"Zoey!"

Zoey, Lola, and Nicole looked up. Quinn was leaning over the balcony above them. The flowers on her pale green shirt matched the blooming vines all around her. But her face was not so sweet. She looked mad.

"I cannot believe you made that commercial!" Quinn yelled.

"What commercial?" Zoey had no idea what Quinn was talking about. And judging from the looks on their faces, neither did Lola or Nicole.

"The one you made about Chase. They keep running it on the school station," Quinn explained huffily.

Zoey crossed her arms and leaned on the wooden table. "What?" she asked again.

"Come look!" Quinn whirled around and marched into the building. The other girls gathered up their bags to follow.

When Zoey got inside, the ad was already running on the large-screen TV in the lounge.

"Chase Matthews wants to be your class president," the voiceover began. A bad picture of the candidate in question filled the screen. "But how well do you really know Chase Matthews?" the voice continued. "For example, did you know he eats out of garbage cans?" The image changed to show Chase leaning on a campus waste receptacle eating a piece of chicken.

Nicole reared back in horror. Gross! She had no idea.

Zoey could not believe her eyes or her ears.

"Or that he shaves his legs?" the voice continued, and the image changed again. This time a picture of Chase with his leg propped up and covered in shaving cream appeared.

Lola's jaw dropped and she looked at Nicole. Was she seeing the same thing? And the commercial was not over. The next picture showed Chase stealing a stuffed bunny from an unsuspecting kid.

"Or that he picks on little girls?" the voice asked. "Is this the kind of guy you want for class president? No!"

A red circle with a line through it slammed down over a picture of Chase. Then the image changed one last time. This time Zoey's face appeared. She was dressed in a tangerine-orange shirt and smiling broadly. "On Tuesday, vote Zoey Brooks for class president. She's awesome."

Quinn whirled and stared at Zoey, waiting for her to defend herself. Zoey was flabbergasted.

"How could you make a mean commercial like that about him?" Nicole asked. She sounded like she was about to burst into tears. Zoey and Chase were like best friends!

"I didn't," Zoey insisted. This was the first time she'd even seen the ad!

Melissa, Chase's number one fan, saw the whole thing. Marching up to Zoey, she stopped right in her face. The lisper was wearing a Chase pin on her striped green polo shirt, and she did not look happy. "Zoey, you have thlandered and dethecrated Chathe'th reputation. That'th thad," she splattered all over Zoey's cheek. "Tho, tho thad."

"All right," Zoey said, wiping spittle off her cheek. She'd heard and felt enough. "Excuse me." She pushed past Melissa and stormed out of the lounge in search of an explanation.

As she combed the campus for her best guy friend, Zoey looked totally fierce. Not just because her folded-up capri jeans, embellished pink cotton tank, and short-sleeve black tie shrug with the Indian print looked slamming on her. No. The outfit was cute. The look on Zoey's face was ferocious.

"Have you guys seen Chase?" Zoey asked a couple of kids she knew from English. She wanted to find Chase now and get to the bottom of the smear campaign. Whoever was behind the cruel ad had some serious explaining to do.

The kids she asked shook their heads and glared at Zoey. "No," the guy said. "But we saw your commercial."

"That was pretty low," his friend added.

"Yeah, yeah," Zoey sighed and walked away. Everyone thought *she* was behind the mean ad. As if. She would never do anything like that to Chase — and if he was thinking she had done it, too . . . Zoey picked up her pace. She would find Chase if she had to search the whole campus!

"Logan!" Zoey spotted Logan talking to a couple of guys under a palm tree. She marched up to him, grabbed him by the elbow, and pulled him out of his conversation. "Where's Chase?" she demanded.

Logan glowered and wagged his finger in Zoey's face. "Hey, that commercial is out of control," he said accusingly. Logan had to admit, there were not many depths that he would not sink to. But he expected more from Zoey.

"Where's Chase?" Zoey demanded again. She struggled to keep herself from yelling. If even Logan thought she had made the commercial, her reputation was already shot.

"He's in his room." Logan shrugged. What was her deal? "Why?"

Zoey walked off without answering. And when she got to Chase's room she didn't bother to knock. She walked in, spotted Chase's curly head on the couch, and slammed the door. "I didn't do it," she said the second he looked up.

"You mean the commercial. . . ." Chase looked confused, and remarkably calm for a guy accused of eating trash, shaving his legs, and being mean to little girls.

"Yes, look, even though I was kind of mad at you, I swear I would never do anything mean like that." Zoey gave Chase a pleading look, desperately hoping he would believe her.

"I know," Chase said calmly.

"Because your friendship means *way* more to me than this dumb election," Zoey went on. She was too worked up to really hear what Chase was saying.

"I made it." Chase pointed at himself.

"And when I find out who made it, I'm gonna hurt 'em," Zoey kept going off.

Finally Chase stood up. He had to stop her. "I made the commercial," he said again, more loudly.

This time Zoey shut up. "Why?" she asked, brushing her thick blond hair away from her face. What could have possessed him?

"Because, I mean, I never wanted to be president," Chase said a little sheepishly. "Look, when I nominated you it was because I really thought that you were the best person for the job." Zoey was squinting at him like he was nuts. "And I still think that," he added. "But I was gonna win because Logan was out of control and it wasn't right. You should be president. That's why I made the commercial." Chase waited for Zoey to tell him thank you. He might even get a hug out of this.

Taking a step forward, Zoey socked Chase in the arm, hard.

"Ow!" Chase grabbed his arm where he took the hit. Where was the love? "What was that?" he asked, baffled.

"Everybody thinks I made it!" Zoey said loudly.

"They do?" Chase asked, still rubbing the sore spot.

"Yes, now the whole school feels bad for you and they hate me." Zoey was so mad she couldn't even look at her friend anymore. Of all the lamebrained schemes!

Spinning around, she ran out the door and slammed it behind her.

"I've been punched." Chase stood in his room alone, holding his blooming bruise. His arm hurt, but not as much as his stomach. His plan had completely back-fired.

CHAPTER 8

News Flash

From the other side of the glass, Zoey looked in at her friends hanging out in the student lounge. Lola and Quinn were playing cards on the maroon polka-dot couch, smiling and talking easily. The TV was on, but nobody was paying much attention. Nicole had her books open at one of the café tables nearby. Everyone looked happy. Zoey felt miserable.

Mustering up her courage — it wasn't easy being the Big Meanie on Campus — Zoey stepped inside. "Hey," she said, pulling up a chair near Nicole.

"Hey," Nicole answered as she looked the other way.

"You wanna go get some dinner? We can go to Sushi Rox or something," Zoey suggested. She needed to get her mind off the whole election mess.

Nicole shifted uncomfortably in her chair before

answering. "Um . . ." She stalled, stood up, and pulled Zoey to a quieter corner of the lounge. "I don't think I should," she said, nervously looking around to see if anyone was watching them.

"I didn't make that commercial," Zoey said. If her best friend and roommate didn't believe her, who would?

"I believe you," Nicole reassured her, "but everyone else thinks you did. And they kinda hate you for it."

Zoey rolled her eyes. *Tell me something I don't know,* she thought.

"And if I hang out with you in public? They'll hate me, too!" Nicole said. She was practically in tears. It wasn't easy choosing between your friend and the rest of the school. "And that makes me really nervous," she babbled. "'Cause I do not handle being hated well at all."

"Can we have sushi together in a closet?" Nicole suggested. She wanted to hang with Zo', just not where anyone else could see her.

"I'm not eating raw fish in a closet." Zoey shook her head sadly. She was down, but that was a completely depressing idea.

Suddenly a loud voice on the TV grabbed the attention of every kid in the room. "We interrupt our usual PCA programming for this special report," the voice announced. Zoey and Nicole stepped closer. Standing behind the couch Quinn and Lola were sitting on, they watched the screen.

A student reporter with a mic appeared behind the BREAKING NEWS banner. His report was live and on campus.

"I'm Jeremiah Trottman," the kid in the tie began smoothly. "It seems that ninth-grade presidential candidate Chase Matthews has called a press conference to make an important announcement. We take you now live to this historic event." Jeremiah stood, still looking into the camera. Behind him a few curious onlookers stared at the camera. "We take you now live to this historic event," Jeremiah repeated through clenched teeth. There was another pause. Then the reporter lost it. "CUT TO THE HISTORIC EVENT!" he shrieked.

The screen changed and Chase appeared. He was standing at a podium in front of a crowd. A PCA banner hung behind him.

"Hi." Chase tapped the mic. "Is this on? Are we on?" he asked over the feedback whine. "Okay." He cleared his throat.

Zoey squinted at the screen. She didn't know how to feel. Lately every time she saw Chase, things got worse. Her stomach was in knots.

"Hi," Chase said again. "My name's Chase Matthews. Or most of you may know me as the guy that eats out of garbage cans, shaves his legs, and picks on little girls. Now, I know that most of you thought that my opponent Zoey Brooks made that commercial. But she didn't. I did," Chase confessed.

The news hit the kids in the student lounge like a ton of bricks.

Lola's mouth dropped open in surprise and she looked at Quinn to make sure she wasn't imagining this. Quinn was staring openmouthed at the screen, too.

It wasn't news to Zoey, but she was still speechless.

"I know that sounds pretty stupid," Chase went on, "but I did it because I really think that Zoey's the best person for the job." He looked directly into the camera when he spoke.

Zoey felt like Chase was looking right at her. She couldn't help but smile a little.

"Which is also why I've decided to drop out of the race for class president," Chase said.

Zoey and Nicole exchanged a look. What was Chase doing?

"Anyway, I guess that's it," Chase finished. "Is the camera off? Yes? It's not off?" Chase stood awkwardly on the podium for another minute. "Well, turn it off!" The cameraman kept rolling and Chase left the frame with a shrug. The girls in the lounge giggled.

"How cute is he?" Nicole turned to Zoey. She had a look on her face that she only got for puppies and guys of the adorable variety. Zoey could only nod. Pretty darn cute, she had to admit. Not to mention brave, and a great friend.

May the Best
Man Win

"Boo!" Zoey found Chase lounging on the rooftop patio of the guys' dorm. The place was done up with Astroturf, fake rocks, and sand, and pink flamingos — it was a great place to go when you wanted to be alone, above the crowd. It reminded Zoey of a mini-golf course. And right about where the first hole would be sat Chase on a lounge chair, wearing shades, sipping water, and apparently studying. A folder was open on his lap.

"Oh." Chase looked up, surprised. "Hi. How'd you find me up here?"

"Do you not want me up here?" Zoey asked, sounding a little hurt.

"No. No." That wasn't what he meant at all. He had just been putting his foot in it so often he was trying to spare Zoey any more of the grief that came with being his friend. But honestly, he was thrilled she was there.

"My roof is your roof. Sit." He indicated the multicolored lounge chair next to his. Zoey slipped off her pack and sat down.

"Orange wedge?" Chase offered. A peeled orange was sitting on the low table next to him along with a bottle of water and a cup with colored balls of ice.

"Sure." Zoey accepted the wedge and took a bite. "Mmm. Good orange."

"Yeah," Chase agreed. "It's sweet."

Zoey almost rolled her eyes. What were they doing discussing an orange?

They both spoke at once.

"Look, I'm really sorry —"

"I'm sorry —"

Then stopped.

"Wait, you're sorry?" Chase asked. What did Zoey have to be sorry about? The guys she scared in the locker room were probably fine by now. "Why are you sorry?" he asked again.

"'Cause this whole week I've been getting mad at you for stuff that was Logan's fault. And I'm really sorry."

Chase nodded. "No problem," he said.

Zoey felt relieved. "So what were you sorry for?" she asked.

"I don't know," Chase admitted. "When a girl gets mad at you, it just seems like the smartest thing to say."

Laughing, Zoey popped the last bit of orange into her mouth. "Very true."

"Yeah." Chase felt relieved, too. He finally had the old Zo' back. Things almost felt like normal.

"So, why'd you drop out of the race?" Zoey asked with a smile.

"Well, after my fabulous smear campaign against myself backfired, I figured getting out of the race was the only way to make sure that you won."

Chase was looking at Zoey from under his shaggy bangs, kind of apologetically. "So I dropped out," he finished.

"Me too," Zoey said with a shrug.

"Yeah, I just — wait." Chase stopped and looked at Zoey. She was completely relaxed and smiling on her lounger. Had he heard her right? "You dropped out?" he asked. "When?"

"This afternoon. Right before you did," Zoey replied.

"But why?"

"Same reason as you." Zoey could not stop smiling. She hadn't felt this good since before she was nominated. "And because I think our friendship is way more important than this stupid election."

Chase let it sink in. The girl had a good point. They were both out of the running. "Well, wait a sec. If I dropped out and you dropped out . . ."

"Oh, yeah." Zoey saw right where Chase's mind was going and asked the question they both wanted the answer to: "Who's going to be president?"

Standing at the PCA podium in the large outdoor amphitheater, PCA's ninth-grade president looked more portly than passionate. "Thank you. Thank you, one and all," he said unenthusiastically. "I, Mark Del Figgalo, will be the best president any ninth-grade class has ever known." Unsmiling, he went on addressing the stands. "I could not have won this election without the support of each and every one of you." The small crowd of three erupted in applause. Quinn, of course, clapped loudest for her guy. The two students behind her did their best to match her enthusiasm. It wasn't easy, especially since one of the supporters was wearing a neck brace that made clapping painful.

"No. No. Please." Mark put up a hand to protest the underwhelming response.

Back on the roof patio, Zoey and Chase leaned on the railing and checked out the PCA campus. The view was great. The new president was decided, but more important, the election was behind them and everything had turned out okay. Everyone had gotten what he or she wanted or deserved. Everyone except . . .

"There's Logan on his skateboard," Zoey pointed out with a devilish look in her eye.

"Oh, yeah." Chase watched Logan swoop closer in his red helmet, remembering all of the stunts he'd pulled over the last few days.

Zoey and Chase looked at each other. Without a word, they knew they were both thinking the same thing, again.

"On three?" Chase asked.

"Count it." Zoey grinned.

"One . . . two . . . three!"

"LOGAN!" Chase and Zoey shouted together before ducking behind the wall.

Logan looked around to see where the voices were coming from. Distracted, he lost his footing on his board and went down on the paved walk. Mortified, he picked himself up.

While Zoey and Chase peeked over the edge of the roof, Logan checked to see that nobody who mattered saw him fall. He was okay, mostly. He would have a bruise, but not on his knee — just on his super-size ego.

CHAPTER
10
Turf War

"I can't believe I have two tests tomorrow," Zoey griped. The election had faded like a temporary tattoo and left Zoey with more important things to think about — like serious relaxation. If only she didn't have schoolwork hanging over her head, she could get down to some serious sunbathing. The guys' rooftop patio was perfect for it. They had the cool Astroturf, the flamingos, the lounge chairs, and Zoey had her new pink-and-white Hawaiian-print tankini top and orange surf shorts.

Two lounge chairs away, Lola was on the same wave of homework avoidance. "Yeah, well, I have to turn in a ten-page paper. And I haven't even started yet." She did not look worried in the least as she flipped the page of her fashion magazine.

Not to be topped, Nicole chimed in, too. "Yeah?

Well, I have more homework than both of you put together," she complained.

"Hey, pass the suntan lotion, would ya?" Zoey asked.

"Sure." Nicole smiled and handed over the tube. "You know," she said, suddenly having a pang of conscience, "we really should be studying."

"Yeah, we should," Zoey agreed, smearing sun-block on her arms.

"*So* should." Lola nodded. She had her hair pulled back in thick braids and held with colored bands that matched her pink, yellow, and green bandeau bikini top.

"But we're just going to stay here and lie in the sun, right?" Nicole asked. She hoped so. The thought of putting her pink rhinestone-dotted two-piece back in a dark drawer depressed her.

"Absolutely," Lola assured her.

"Thank goodness," Nicole sighed. Ever since Zoey discovered the guys' roof patio it was the only place Nicole, Zoey, and Lola wanted to be. It was heaven at PCA.

"Hey," a less friendly voice interrupted the girls' chill time. "What are you people doing up on our roof?" Logan ambled up to the sunbathers sounding completely annoyed. When the girls didn't answer, Logan turned to Chase, who was right behind him. "What are they doing on our roof?" he demanded.

"They appear to be lying on chairs," Chase replied, stating the obvious.

"*Our* chairs!" Logan snarled.

"Why are you all cranky?" Lola asked, looking up from her gossip mag. She raised her sunglasses and gave Logan a quizzical look.

"Someone hide your mirror?" Zoey teased as she leaned back on her towel.

Nicole and Lola cracked up.

"Funny," Logan said sarcastically. "Now get off our roof." He jerked his thumb back toward the stairs.

"Noooo." Nicole scrunched up her face. Was he kidding? He was not the boss of her!

"We're not bothering you," Lola said.

"Why should we have to leave?" Zoey asked.

"Because." Logan thought the girls had some nerve. He and Chase had come to the roof to chill. To hang out. To get away from it all. Not to be with girls. "This is the guys' dorm." He pointed down at the building they were on. "Which means this roof is for guys only."

Whatever. Zoey'd heard enough of Logan's complaining. "Chase, tell Logan he's being an idiot." At least she could count on Chase to be reasonable.

"Actually?" Chase could not believe what he was about to say, but . . . "I kind of agree with him."

"Huh?"

"Chase!"

Lola and Nicole sat up and stared.

"You're taking Logan's side on this?" Zoey was floored. Just when you thought you knew a guy . . .

"PCA was just a guys' school for a long time," Chase tried to explain. "Then they let girls in, which is great."

"Sometimes," Logan mumbled.

"But I think the guys do kind of need a place where we can just, you know, be guys," Chase finished, crossing his arms over his red T-shirt and hoping the girls would understand.

"Fine." Nicole raised her eyebrows. "So just pull up a chair and burp. We don't care."

"Guys can't just be guys with girls around." Logan had cut the arms off of his Stingrays Basketball sweatshirt so that it would show off his muscular tanned arms. And he was ready to work on his tan — if he could get the girls off his roof already.

"Why not?" Lola asked.

"Because when females hang around males, it just causes the males to behave differently," Chase explained. "We can't help it."

"It's basic biology," Logan said seriously. He was acting like some sort of nature expert.

"You got a C minus in biology," Zoey pointed out.

Snap! Lola held up a hand and waited to see how Logan was going to respond to *that*.

"Yeah?" he asked defensively, putting his hands on his hips. "Well, who was the best-looking guy in class, huh? Yeah," he answered his own question as he gazed off into the distance. "Me." And that was all that really mattered.

"Uh." Chase cleared his throat. "I was in that class," he said softly.

"What's your point?" Logan squinted at Chase. The guy did not seriously think he was in the same league as —

"Okay," Lola interrupted the bickering, "I admit, guys do act differently when girls are around, but it's not because of nature or biology."

"Right," Nicole agreed. "It's 'cause of dumbness and stupidity."

"There you go." Zoey gave her girls their due,

then turned back to the guys. "Now, why don't you be nice boys and go fix us some more lemonade?" Zoey waved her glass. It was empty and she was parched.

"Nu-uh," Logan scowled at them. "Leave," he ordered, pointing to the stairs a second time.

Zoey did not like being told what to do. Especially not by Logan. "No," she shot back as she crossed her arms.

"Uh-oh." Nicole caught the gesture. Things were about to get heated. "She crossed her arms," she cautioned the boys. And when Zoey crossed her arms, things happened.

"It's on." Lola smiled. She loved a good fight. She crossed her arms in solidarity with her girl Zoey.

"*So* on." Nicole picked Lola's magazine up to wait for the show.

"Fine, then I'll just go tell our dorm advisor to *make* you leave our roof," Logan threatened.

"Then I'll talk to him, too," Zoey said, grabbing her maroon tank and flip-flops.

"Me, too." Nicole got her own stuff. She was not about to miss this! And the two girls stormed after Logan to go talk to the guys' D.A.

Chase looked around, not quite sure what had happened. Lola went back to her mag. "Hey," she said when she noticed Chase just standing there with nothing to do. "Can you turn up the music?" She pointed toward her cute new turquoise boom box balanced on the ledge of the roof.

"Yeah, sure." Chase shrugged. He wasn't anxious to go join in the fight that was sure to be starting downstairs. And as much as he didn't want the girls on the roof, he was not about to kick Lola off her towel. Especially since she brought the tunes.

"Hey, cool boom box," Chase said admiringly.

"Thanks. I just got it." Lola smiled.

Chase looked closer, trying to find the volume. He reached out and pushed one of the tiny buttons . . . and the whole box slid over the edge of the roof. Chase watched it fall, almost like it was traveling in slow motion. Then he saw it smash to pieces on the cement below.

"Was it expensive?" Chase asked nervously. He had a feeling he was going to be in the market for one just like it, pronto.

Seeing Spots

Standing in the dorm advisor's room, Zoey, Logan, and Nicole were all screaming at once. It was hard to hear anything, but the tall blond D.A. they were screaming at had already heard enough.

"Okay," he shouted. "Okay, all right. Cool it." If the advisor was going to help work this out, he needed to get some things straight. "So why can't you girls hang out on your own roof?" he asked.

"'Cause our roof's lame," Zoey told him.

"Yeah. It doesn't get any sun, it has bugs, and there's a tree above it with a bunch of squirrels so it smells like squirrel pee," Nicole elaborated on the lameness. Nobody could be expected to hang out on a roof like that (except the bugs and squirrels).

"PCA used to be just for guys only," Logan jumped to his own defense. It didn't matter what the girls' roof was like. He couldn't care less. Let them hang out in a basement. "Now the roof is the last place we've got that's just for us." Logan looked at the D.A. hard. The dude had to understand his point.

And he did. "Girls, the roof is part of the boys' dorm, so if they want to keep it private, I think they have a right to."

"Ha!" Logan "ha'd" in their faces. "Later, losers," he mocked before walking out.

Zoey laughed at Logan's jerkish behavior, then stepped closer to the older blond guy. "Okay," she said to the D.A. reasonably. "If we can't go on their roof, then they can't come in the girls' lounge anymore."

"Uh, yes they can." Nicole stepped up beside Zoey, grabbing her arm and smiling at the advisor.

"Nicole?" Zoey looked at Nicole like she was out of her head. Why was she contradicting her here?

Nicole ignored her friend. She had to act quickly. This was an emergency situation. "This conversation's over. You're free to go now," she gave the advisor her best flight attendant smile and hoped he would move about the cabin.

The dorm advisor rolled his eyes and walked away, eager to be done with the whole business.

"Why did you do that?" Zoey demanded when he

was gone. Didn't Nicole see that it was unfair for them to share their space when the guys refused to do the same?

"'Cause I like guys hanging out in the girls' lounge," Nicole said. Then she broke it down for Zoey the best way she knew how. "That lounge is my ice cream and boys are the sprinkles," she stated matter-of-factly.

"Whatever," Zoey sighed. Nicole was letting her boy-craziness get the better of her. What about justice? What about getting back to those lounge chairs on the guys' roof?

"I've got to go see Dustin," Zoey sighed again. She would deal with the roof issue later.

"Okay, I'll come with you," Nicole said, starting to follow.

"He's in the infirmary with chicken pox," Zoey cautioned.

As Zoey could have predicted, Nicole's tune changed abruptly. "Bye. Have fun." She waved good-bye and quickly disappeared out the door. Itchy scarring diseases were not her best thing.

"Knock, knock." After tapping softly on the frame of the door, Zoey stepped inside the school infirmary.

Dustin was awake, spotted and scratching, stretched out on one of the beds in the large sickroom.

"Oh, hi, Zo'," her little brother greeted with a smile. Except for the red spots all over his face and arms, he was as cute as ever with his shaggy blond hair and big brown eyes.

Zoey was glad she was bringing the kid good news. "So I talked to your roommate's mom. Turns out he's already had the chicken pox." She sat down on the foot of Dustin's bed, smiling. "You don't have to stay here in the infirmary anymore!"

"Um, thanks," Dustin said. He didn't look as thrilled as Zoey had expected. "But I think I should stay a couple more days."

"But if you feel okay why would you want to stay in the infirmary?" Zoey asked. The place was pretty sterile. And she had heard stories about the nurse.

"I, uh." Dustin squirmed. Just then, the answer to Dustin's dreams walked in carrying a vanilla cone.

"Hey, Dustin," the pretty brunette in scrubs cooed.

"Hey, Shannon." Dustin beamed at the young woman.

"Who's Shannon?" Zoey whispered. Whoever she was, it was pretty clear Dustin had a major crush!

"My nurse," Dustin whispered back. Then he introduced them. "Shannon, this is my sister, Zo'."

"Hi." Shannon smiled at Zoey. She seemed really nice. "Thought you might like a little ice cream," she said to Dustin as she handed over the sugar cone.

"You thought right!" Dustin took the ice cream excitedly. "Again!" Shannon had a way of reading his mind — fluffing pillows at the right moment, bringing him water when he needed it, and she was genius with calamine. She had a caregiving gift. Not to mention the fact that she was beautiful.

"Oh, Dustin." Shannon smiled sweetly at the compliment.

Zoey watched the whole scene, suddenly understanding her little brother's reluctance to go. Dustin had a good thing going and she didn't want to mess it up. "Well, I'll leave you two alone," she said as she got to her feet.

"Wait! Before you go, can you take a picture of me and Shannon with your phone?" Dustin asked.

"Sure." Zoey fished her phone out of her round blue-striped bag and aimed it at the pair, nurse and patient, mugging in front of Dustin's pillow. "Say 'pox,'" she prompted.

"Pox!" they said and smiled in unison.

Zoey snapped the pic.

"Okay. I'll check on you in a few minutes," Shannon reassured her patient. "Pleased to meet you, Zoey," she said.

"Yeah, you too," Zoey agreed. "So, who do you want me to send this picture to?" she asked her brother when Shannon was gone. He probably wanted to brag to his roommate about his gorgeous nurse.

"Everyone!" Dustin grinned.

CHAPTER 12

Perfect Plan

Sitting on a lounge chair in her green patterned bikini, Nicole pulled off her shades. There was no point in wearing them here. There was no sun, and even if there was, it would be blocked by the tall electrified fence that protected the horrible-looking and enormous satellite dish in one corner. "I hate our roof," Nicole fumed. "I hate it so much!"

In the striped lounge chair next to Nicole, Lola had to agree. "It gets, like, no sun," she complained before biting into her apple. At least that was good. But what was the point of lying out in her embroidered black two-piece in the *shade*?

"Yeah, I think I'm actually getting whiter." Zoey held out her arm and stared at it. It definitely looked paler.

Lola sat up and wrinkled her nose. "And it smells like squirrel pee," she noted.

"See? I'm not crazy." Nicole was glad she was not the only one sensitive to the scent of rodent urine.

"Hey, you know what?" Zoey swung her feet over the edge of the lounge chair onto the nasty stick-in-your-toes rocks that covered the roof. She didn't even notice the uncomfortable stones. She was having an idea. An idea that might get them back on the guys' superior-sunning roof.

"What?" Nicole asked.

Lola looked up.

"Maybe we ought to prove to Chase and Logan that guys can be just guys even when girls are around," Zoey suggested.

It was a great idea, but . . . "How are we going to do that?" Lola wondered.

"By being around them when they don't know we're around." Zoey had a twinkle in her eye. They were going to be back in the sun on the guys' roof before they knew it!

Nicole was confused. Her eyebrows were furrowed. "But if we're around trying to prove it, we'll be around them and we're girls so they'll be around girls when we're trying to —"

"Maybe you should let Zoey talk," Lola suggested before smoke started pouring out of Nicole's ears.

Zoey smiled. Nicole was making it hard, but really it was simple. "I'm saying, what if one of us pretends to be a guy?"

"Okay," Nicole said, sounding totally unconvinced. Zoey was missing some pretty obvious stuff. "Several problems with that: hair, face, body."

Zoey was still smiling. "We can get around those problems," she said, nodding slowly.

"It *would* be the ultimate acting challenge," Lola said, catching Zoey's twinkle. "And I *am* the ultimate actress." She could see right where this was headed and she was up for it!

Only Nicole was still skeptical. "You really think you can convince Chase and Logan that you're a guy?" she asked, looking at her thespian roomie.

"Easy," Lola assured her. "Chase is gullible and Logan's a moron."

Nicole had to admit Lola had some good points.

"But if we're gonna do this right," Zoey said, still plotting, "then we're gonna need a little inside help."

Zoey's "inside help" came in the form of one tall, cute, roommate. Namely, Michael Barrett. Zoey caught up to him the next day walking to class and filled him in on the girls' plan.

"Whoa, whoa, whoa, whoa." Michael needed Zoey to slow down. She was talking fast and he wanted to get this straight. "Lola's gonna pretend to be a guy?" he asked. "I can think of three problems with that."

"Don't worry about them," Zoey said. They were taken care of. "So, will you help us?" she asked, smoothing her black tee with its tattoo-esque peace design.

"Uh . . . make a fool out of my roommates . . ." Michael paused and fiddled with the strap of the bright orange messenger bag on his shoulder. He looked like he was really agonizing over the decision. Then suddenly his tune changed. "Sure!" He tossed up his hands. Of course he would. How could he miss a chance to humiliate Chase and Logan? "What do you want me to do?" he asked.

Zoey grinned. Michael was in! "Okay, first you help us turn Lola into a believable guy. You'll be sort of like our guy consultant."

"Okay." It sounded easy to Michael so far.

"And you can't stay in your room for a couple of days." Zoey squinched up her nose. This was the tricky part. She knew Michael might need some convincing for this. Luckily she had all the tools she needed in her pocket.

"Why not?" Michael asked.

"'Cause we're gonna make Lola the new temporary roommate," Zoey explained.

"And where am I supposed to sleep?" Michael asked.

Easy. Zoey had it all worked out. "You pretend to be sick, and you sleep in the infirmary." They had plenty of extra beds.

"Oh, no. Nuh-uh." Michael shook his head. He had been going to PCA for a long time and so far he had successfully avoided that place. "I heard about Nurse Krutcher," he told Zoey. The woman was mean and strong, and she enjoyed dishing up pain. Chase had a run-in with her and almost didn't survive it.

"No! They have a new nurse," Zoey assured Michael.

Michael did not look convinced.

"Wanna see her?" Zoey asked playfully.

"O-okay," Michael reluctantly agreed.

Zoey pulled her secret weapon out of her pocket and flashed Michael the shot she took of Dustin and Shannon on her camera phone. Michael stared. "Well?" she asked.

"Well . . ." Michael put his hand to his forehead. The new nurse was a knockout. "I think I'm coming down with a fever!" he exclaimed.

CHAPTER 13

Extreme Makeover

"Okay, Lola." Nicole spun Lola around in one of the swivel chairs in the student lounge and gave her a once-over. Even dressed in a guyish seventies-style ringer T-shirt with a Capricorn horoscope logo on the front she looked way too pretty to be a boy. Her long, green-tipped brown hair was going to be hard to hide — and so were her delicate features and pretty eyes. Not to mention the other problems. But it was now or never.

"You ready to become a guy?" Zoey asked, spinning Lola back to look at her.

"Yup!" Lola grinned at Zoey, Nicole, and Michael, who was crashed on the couch as she spun. "Make me a dude!"

They had already gathered all of the theatrical supplies they needed. Now it was just a matter of applying them. The four ran up to the room the girls shared, pulled Lola's hair back in a ponytail, and got started with some makeup. Zoey did most of the application. She made Lola's skin ruddier and gave her some freckles.

Nicole dug through the cosmetic bags. It was a shame they could not use the sparkling pink eye shadow. But hey, bonus! At least she'd located her favorite blush. She thought she left it in the lockers.

While the girls made Lola up, Michael yacked on his cell. He didn't know much about makeup. But he did know about guys. When Zoey got heavy-handed with the blush, Michael made her tone it down. And when they were almost done, he came up with the ultimate guy accessory — a mustache — and stuck it on.

Zoey and Nicole made faces. Lola wiggled her furry lip uncomfortably. Michael thought it looked fantastic. But Nicole shoved Michael back and onto Zoey's bed while Zoey yanked the fur flap off (along with quite a bit of Lola's upper lip skin!).

Next they put Lola in a boy suit they borrowed from Theater Arts. It was totally convincing and had a wide chest pad to resemble muscles. Lola wasn't just a guy, she was a buff guy!

Now it was time to pick clothes. The first outfit, a short-sleeve button-down shirt with a big green-and-yellow-plaid print made Lola look like a dork. The next outfit, layered dark polos with too-big pleated khakis, was worse. Ugh!

The last outfit was the clear winner — a white long-sleeve under an army-green distressed T-shirt with patches and red-and-white stripes sewn on the shoulders. With some loose jeans and a pair of big black boots, she looked just like the skater kids Logan hung out with. Except she still had a ponytail.

It was hair time. Nicole put the selection of three wigs mounted on Styrofoam heads on the dresser. They had a red curly one, a blond shaggy one, and a brown one. Lola tried them one at a time. The red one was like a bad cross between Little Orphan Annie and Ronald McDonald. The blond one was worse — it was helmet hair for sure. So that left the brown one.

Zoey held her breath as Lola tugged it on over the stocking that held her real hair in place. And . . . it looked great! Lola was a dude!

"Well?" Lola stood up and spoke in a deep voice. She crossed her arms and let Zoey, Nicole, and Michael take a good look. The team applauded.

"Unbelievable!" Zoey exclaimed.

"I could almost date you!" Nicole said, impressed.

"Come here, baby." Lola the dude made kissy

faces at Nicole, who bent over backward to avoid the "new guy."

"N-n-n-n-no." Nicole held her arms up. "Back off, boy."

Zoey laughed. She felt proud of the way Lola had turned out. They all seemed pretty convinced. Only Michael still hadn't said anything. "Michael, what do you think?" Zoey asked. After all, he was the only bona fide boy in the mix.

"It's good," Michael said, squinting at Lola. "But I still vote for the mustache." He held up the scrap of hair and glue.

Nicole pushed Michael's arm down. "Yeah, well, it's time for you to stop voting and go check into the infirmary," she said as she herded him toward the door.

"But don't you think this mustache would help the overall look of Lola's whole —"

Nicole closed the door before Michael finished his sentence. "He had to go," she said, leaning on the door. There was no way she was going to let him put a mustache on their work of art!

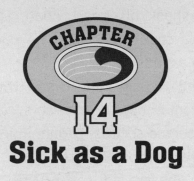

Sick as a Dog

When Michael arrived at the infirmary he was working it. The cool thing was, he had convinced Chase and Logan that he was sick. He had one of his friends on each arm, looking at him all worried — like he might expire right there. If he had them going, convincing that new nurse was going to be a piece of cake.

"Man, you sound awful," Logan said. He actually sounded concerned.

From his bed, Dustin set down the Hatman comic he was reading and watched the guys come in. "What's wrong with Michael?" he asked Chase. Michael was staggering and coughing and holding his ribs.

"We don't know," Chase said, putting a hand on Michael's shoulder. "Dude, you sure you don't want to stay in your own bed, in our dorm?" he asked. When *he* was sick, he liked to be where he was comfortable.

Michael shook his head. "Nah. I think I oughta hang here for a couple of days," he panted. "Where's the nurse?" he asked.

"Shannon!" Dustin called, and the pretty nurse stepped out from behind a privacy screen. She looked great in light purple scrubs. Logan, Chase, and Michael all took an awed step backward.

"Whoa," Chase said softly. She was gorgeous. "When did you start working at PCA?" Chase asked in his best smooth-talking voice.

"About a month ago," Shannon answered, looking at the guys with concern. "Is one of you sick?"

Michael coughed again and collapsed on Chase's shoulder, moaning.

"Yeah, Michael here," Logan said, patting his friend on the shoulder.

"I can barely stand." Michael staggered between Logan and Chase. Then he held his arms out to Shannon. "Help me," he begged.

"Of course!" Shannon put an arm around Michael and he collapsed onto her.

"So soft," Michael mumbled as he stroked Shannon's arm.

"Well, I'd say you're in good hands." Chase raised

his eyebrows at Michael. Maybe he would come to the infirmary next time he was sick, too. . . .

"Very good hands," Logan added.

Michael coughed and groaned happily.

"Well, feel better, man." Chase patted Michael and turned to go.

"I'll try," Michael said pitifully and waved his friends off. The sooner they were gone, the sooner nurse Shannon could start taking care of him.

"You poor thing," Shannon cooed.

"Thank you." Michael made his way toward a bed. "I'm just glad I have you to take care of me."

"Oh, I won't be taking care of you," Shannon corrected Michael, pulling away from him to look in his face.

Michael stood up straight and stopped coughing. "What do you mean?" he asked.

"Shannon's the nurse for the lower-school kids," Dustin explained from his bed.

Michael tried not to panic. "But I was told that —"

Suddenly the infirmary door opened again and a large woman dressed in scrubs stomped in. "Stupid Taco Hut!" she bellowed, glaring at her fast-food bag. "I ask for a nacho bean-and-cheese burrito and they give me all bean!" Her voice made Michael's knees weak. It was nurse Krutcher! She slammed her bag on the desk so hard, Michael thought he was having a heart attack.

"What's wrong with this one?" Krutcher asked, turning around and eyeing Michael like she hadn't just had a total tantrum.

"He's very sick," Shannon answered.

"A-actually, I feel much better." Michael patted Shannon's arm. It was time for a miraculous recovery — and a hasty exit!

"Lay down," Krutcher barked.

Michael started to protest. "Seriously, I —"

"LAY DOWN!" the big woman bellowed.

Michael shrieked like a toddler and lay down right on the floor. Scrambling backward like a crab, he reached a bed. "Cheese and rice," Michael swore. He pulled himself up on the mattress and clutched the pillow he found there like it was a life preserver. He did not dare take his eyes off the nurse. There was no telling what she would do if he did not obey!

"I love my job." Krutcher smiled briefly at Shannon before cracking her beefy knuckles. Her grimacelike smile still plastered on her face, she tilted her head to the side until her neck popped like corn and then tossed her shoulders back to snap the vertebrae in her back.

Michael shivered in his bed. The sound was like fire-crackers . . . only scary.

Carefully Quinn made the last adjustments to her latest project. Holding the screwdriver between green-frosted nails, she gave a final turn and . . . "There!" She took the high-tech specs and placed them on Lola's duded-up face. "Your new glasses." Quinn smiled. She loved it when a project came together.

"They won't explode, will they?" Lola asked nervously. Quinn was a genius, but some of her experiments were, uh, volatile, to say the least.

"Probably not," Quinn said with an easy shrug.

Lola was looking for a little more assurance than that. But an actress had to do what she had to do.

"So how do they work?" Zoey asked before taking a swig of Blix. Nicole was sitting next to her on the bed in their dorm. She looked curious about the glasses, too.

"This teeny little thing on the bridge" — Quinn pointed at a small dot right between Lola's eyes — "is a wireless camera with a built-in microphone. And back here on the thingy that goes around her left ear is a tiny speaker." Lola turned so Nicole and Zoey could get a look, but the speaker was completely invisible. Nobody would suspect a thing.

"So with the computer, we can see and hear everything she sees and hears, and she can hear us via this." Quinn held up a short-wave radio handset.

"So, what's the plan?" Lola asked. She was costumed and wired and ready to hit the stage.

"You go to the guys' dorm and show their D.A. the fake letter from Dean Rivers. And then you'll be roomies with Chase and Logan," Zoey explained.

"Right, and with Quinn's glasses we'll be able to see everything you do and say," Nicole said.

"And you can hear us," Quinn added.

"So if you ever get stuck? We'll help you out." Nicole raised her eyebrows at Lola. She was starting to get really excited about their plan, especially the spying part. She could be like Charlie in *Charlie's Angels.*

"You have the letter?" Lola asked.

"Oh, yeah." Quinn reached for the forged note. "Here." She handed it to Lola, but before Lola got a good look Nicole snatched it out of her hands.

"Whoa! It looks so real!" Nicole couldn't get over it. It was printed on three-color PCA letterhead and everything.

Zoey looked over Nicole's shoulder. "How did you make this?" she asked Quinn. It was totally impressive.

"Please," Quinn said. That was nothing! "I have a

high-end computer and a color laser printer. I could make you French money if you wanted."

Ooh-la-la. Nicole tossed her hair. "I *would* like to go shopping in Paris," she said. Her pink linen skirt and pink layered tees with yarn embroidered flowers and matching beads was a great outfit, but who knew what you could find in France? Looking around at the three pairs of rolling eyes, Nicole scowled. "Aw, let me fantasize," she griped.

Nicole could fantasize all she wanted, but Zoey was ready to get their show on the road. "All right, *Steve*," she said, "do you think you're ready to fool Chase and Logan?"

"Yeah, you look like a guy, but can you act like a guy?" Nicole challenged Lola.

With an ultracool, I-couldn't-care-less look on her face, Lola stood up. She casually spit the wad of gum she had been chewing across the room. It landed in the trash can without touching the rim — a perfect shot. Then, turning back to her friends, she let out a four-Blix burp. It was disgusting. And *really* impressive.

"I think she's ready," Zoey said.

"Mmm-hmm." Nicole nodded. Way ready.

CHAPTER

15

Guyish

"Steve" strolled across campus in his baggy jeans, layered T-shirts, and square-framed glasses. It all looked so good, nobody would have guessed it was a costume and that "he" was a she.

"'Sup," she greeted, nodding at a passerby.

"How ya doin?" She slugged another on the shoulder as she passed. Her black-and-blue duffel swung at her hip.

Back in Quinn's room, Quinn typed a few words into her computer keyboard. "Display visual image," she said as she typed. Glancing at her monitor, she sat back and crossed her arms with satisfaction. Now the girls could see "Steve's" every move on Quinn's computer monitor.

"We're seeing exactly what Steve is seeing," Quinn explained proudly.

Nicole dropped her handful of popcorn back into the bowl and leaned toward the screen. "Whoa," she said. It was exactly as if she were walking through the PCA campus!

"That is so cool," Zoey agreed, taking a sip of Blix.

Quinn nodded, her multiple ponytails and braids bobbing. "Oh, here," she said, handing over the walkie-talkie. "Talk to her."

Zoey smiled, took the radio communicator, and pressed the TALK button. "Lola, can you hear me?" she asked.

"Loud and clear," Lola replied. "But call me Steve!" She waved her hands in exasperation. If she was going to be in character, she needed her friends to call her by her character's name!

"Sorry, Steve," Zoey said sheepishly. The least she could do was play along.

"What about her guy voice?" Nicole said, wrinkling her nose. "It's kinda high."

"Hey, how's it goin'?" Steve said, slapping a high five with some kid she barely knew.

"What's up, dog?" She rapped another kid on the back.

Then she spied a couple of girls up ahead. One of them was wearing a totally adorable V-neck tank with angled stripes and sequins. "Oh, my god!" she exclaimed. "That top is sooo cute — where'd you buy it? I love it!"

Zoey punched a button on the talkie. "Steve!" she scolded. "Quit acting all girly!"

Lola did a double take. How did she get out of character so easily? She had to pull it together, fast. "Yo, your shirt rocks," she said in her guy voice, thumping the girl on the shoulder. "Later," she added, trying not to cringe as she strutted away, leaving the two girls staring after her.

Lola tried to ignore the odd looks the girls were giving her as she kept on walking. She'd have to do a lot better than that to fool Chase and Logan!

"All right, just get to the guys' dorm," Zoey instructed over the talkie. She set the receiver down, frustrated. "She almost blew her cover!" she exclaimed, blowing a thick strand of blond hair out of her eyes.

Nicole nodded gravely, but her tone was sympathetic. "It *was* a really cute top," she noted, taking a sip of Blix.

Zoey shot her a look. As if that mattered!

Over in the guys' dorm, the dorm advisor was introducing Steve to Chase and Logan. "So, since Michael is gonna be in the infirmary for a few days, is it cool if Steve bunks with you guys?"

Chase looked up from the electric guitar he was strumming and shrugged. "Sure, why not?"

"Cool with me," Logan added with a casual nod.

"All right, thanks, dudes," Steve said, setting down his bag and giving Logan and Chase a knuckle shake.

The girls grinned as they watched the action on Quinn's monitor. "They bought it!" Quinn said happily.

"All right, we're in!" Zoey said. So far, so good.

"Yay!" Nicole cheered. This was getting exciting.

"Perfect," Quinn agreed. Another experiment that was right on track.

"Okay, I guess I'll check you guys later," the dorm advisor told Chase and Logan as he stepped past Steve and headed out the door.

Chase smiled at his temporary roommate. "So, Steve, Michael's bed is the top bunk over there, if you wanna put your stuff down."

Steve shook his head. "Cool, thanks." He tossed his bag up onto the bed.

"Blix?" Logan offered, opening the beverage-stocked minifridge.

"Sure. Chuck it," Steve replied, holding his hands up ready to catch it.

In Quinn's room, Nicole nodded appreciatively. "Chuck it," she repeated. "Very guyish."

Steve caught the drink, unscrewed the top, and took a sip.

"So, uh, Steve," Logan said, taking his own cold drink over to the sofa and sitting down. "Where ya from?"

"Chicago," Steve replied. "Go, Tigers, whooo!" he added for good measure.

Chase looked up from his guitar with a confused look on his face. "Uh, the Tigers play for Detroit," he pointed out.

Logan shot Steve a look. What kind of guy didn't know his own hometown team? "Yeah, Chicago's team is the Cubs."

"Yeahhh," Steve agreed. "I know." He had to make it sound like he was cheering for some other tigers. "The Tigers at the . . ."

Quinn grabbed the talkie. "The zoo!" she said, thinking fast.

"Uh, the zoo," Steve repeated, feeling like a total dork. Nice suggestion, Quinn! He laughed to try and cover. Were Logan and Chase onto him?

"The zoo?" Logan repeated. Who was this guy?

Steve shook his head. "Uh, I enjoy animals," he confessed, looking down at the bottle in his hand. "And Blix," he added, taking a swig. This was not going smoothly. . . .

Over in the infirmary, Dustin and Nurse Shannon were blowing bubbles. As they blew streams of the shimmery orbs into the air, they giggled together. Dustin couldn't believe his luck. Having the chicken pox was great when you had a beautiful nurse to take care of you. Maybe he could stay in here a few more days. . . .

On the other end of the room, Michael shivered and glared. While Dustin sat cozily blowing bubbles with the most beautiful nurse ever to set foot in the PCA infirmary, he was shivering like a Jell-O snowman in a giant tub of ice!

Standing over him with a scowl, Nurse Krutcher dumped several more cubes into the tub.

"Whhhyyyy mmmuuussst I sssiiitt iiinnn aaa ttttuubbbb oooff iccccce?" Michael asked, shaking uncontrollably.

"To bring your fever down," Nurse Krutcher replied as she dumped the last pieces of ice into the metal tub.

"Buuttt I dddonnn't hhaavvve a fffeevveeer," Michael protested through chattering teeth.

Nurse Krutcher crossed her arms and looked down at Michael sternly. "Then it's working, ain't it?" she asked.

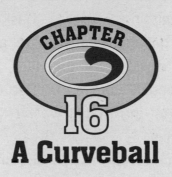

CHAPTER 16

A Curveball

The next morning Logan awoke to the sound of a ringing phone — his phone. He grabbed it off the shelf next to his bed and flipped it open without looking at the number. "Yeah?" he grumbled, wishing he was still asleep. But a second later he was throwing off the covers.

"Oh, man — I totally forgot," he admitted. "Give us fifteen minutes." He scrambled to his feet. Luckily he was pretty much already dressed since he slept in his standard uniform — a tank top and shorts. He scanned the floor for his shoes.

"Chase! Dude!" he shouted, picking up a football off the floor. "Get up!"

Thud! The ball hit Chase square in the back. He sat up, shoved aside his covers, and glared. "Okay, must you be hurling balls my way at . . ." He checked his watch. "Eight o'clock on a Saturday morning?"

"We're missing water basketball," Logan explained, as if getting awoken with a football to the spine was no big deal.

"Ahhh, I forgot." Chase knocked on the top bunk, momentarily forgetting that it wasn't Michael who was sleeping above him.

Steve reached for his glasses and slipped them on her face. "What up?" she asked.

Across campus, Zoey pushed her own red-and-pink floral duvet aside and got out of bed. She'd thought she heard voices. . . . Was she dreaming?

Still yawning, she crossed the room and checked the monitor. No, not dreaming. The guys — Lola being one of them — were already up!

"Nicole, they're up!" she called to her roommate.

She walked over to the wall next to her bed and pounded on it. "Quinn, get in here!" she shouted, pulling her pink jammy top down over her Hawaiian-print bottoms.

Five seconds later all three girls were watching the action on the monitor.

"We can't play water basketball," Chase said, shaking his head.

"Why can't we?" Logan wanted to know.

"Uh, we don't have a full team — Michael's sick."

Logan nodded as he slung a towel around his neck. The dude had a point. "Hey, Steve, you swim, right?" Logan asked, looking pleased. The problem had just come up and already he had a solution.

"Uh, sure, but . . ." Lola panicked. "I don't have swim trunks."

Logan smiled and rifled around in one of his drawers. No problem. "You can wear one of mine." He tossed the trunks to Steve, hitting him smack in the face.

"Come on, we can get changed by the pool," Chase said, grabbing his own trunks and a towel. There was no time to lose.

"Yeah, let's play some water ball!" Logan pumped a fist in the air.

"I really can't," Steve protested. "I have sinus issues and . . ."

Chase grabbed his temporary roommate by the arm. Sinus issues or no, they needed a full team to play! Steve was in.

Filled with panic, Steve followed Chase out the door.

*   *   *

In Zoey's room, the girls stared at the monitor in shock.

"What are we gonna do?" Zoey cried, feeling panic rise. This was not good.

"She can't go swimming," Quinn practically shrieked.

Nicole looked at them, her nose wrinkled in confusion. "Why not?" she asked. "It's gorgeous out!" She gestured out the window to the beautiful Pacific Coast morning.

Zoey grabbed Nicole by the arms and shook her. "What is the matter with you?" she asked. "She's wearing a full boy-body suit!"

Quinn grabbed Nicole and spun her around so fast, her long dark hair went flying. "And a wig and makeup!" she added.

Nicole crossed her arms. "You don't have to get all yelly," she pouted. She got it already.

Zoey grabbed the talkie. "Don't worry, Lola," she said, trying to sound more reassuring than she felt. "We'll figure something out."

The PCA pool was jam-packed with guys warming up for water basketball.

"Hey, guys." Logan greeted his teammates by tilting his chin casually. "We'll be ready in a sec."

"C'mon, let's go get our swim trunks on," Chase said, heading for the guys' locker room.

Lola slipped away from her temporary roommates to talk to her real ones. "Guys, help me!" she whispered, standing at the edge of the pool and trying not to panic. She was still dressed in long pants and a pair of T-shirts. "I can't swim and still pretend to be a guy, if you know what I'm sayin'."

Zoey took a deep breath. "Relax, we've got a plan," she said into the talkie. "Okay, when Chase comes back, just tell him —"

"Dude, come on!" Logan said impatiently, coming up behind Steve. Their temp roommate was quickly becoming a drag.

Logan thumped Steve on the back so hard that his glasses slipped off his face and fell into the water. Steve watched miserably as they slowly sank to the bottom of the pool. The electronic devices fizzled and snapped.

"Uh-oh." Zoey, Nicole, and Quinn all watched in horror as the monitor got all fuzzy, then went black.

"Oh, man," Zoey groaned.

"My teeny camera!" Quinn wailed.

"We'll get you a new teeny camera!" Zoey said, exasperated. The camera was small potatoes. "Right now we gotta get Lola out of swimming!"

"Steve," Nicole corrected.

"I know," Zoey said, irritated.

"Oohhh!" Quinn suddenly said. "I've got an idea!"

"What?" Nicole hoped it was a good one — you could never tell with Quinn.

"Meet me at the swimming pool," she said excitedly. "I've gotta go to my dorm room and get Marvin."

"Marvin?" Nicole repeated, shaking her head. Who the heck was Marvin? Quinn's boyfriend was Mark of the figs. . . .

"Just hurry up and get dressed," Zoey instructed.

In the infirmary, Nurse Krutcher was squeezing Michael's neck with her vicelike grip.

"Ow, ow, ow!" Michael objected as he squirmed on the exam table. "What are you doing?"

"Feeling your glands," the nurse replied flatly before giving up and letting go. "I don't know what's wrong with you," she admitted. She looked sternly at

Michael. "I'm gonna have to take more blood," she said, pulling out a giant needle.

Michael's eyes went wide. "Sweet mother of molasses," Michael murmured. Just when he thought it could not get any worse.

Pool Panic

Things were heating up at the pool. Chase and Logan were both in their swim trunks ready to play, but Steve was still in his clothes, shaking his head no. And the game was already being held up.

"Why not?" Logan asked, shooting Steve a "what is your problem" look. Why couldn't the guy just get in the pool and play?

"You said you could swim," Chase pointed out.

"Uh ... uh ..." Steve stammered. "Did you mean swim like in water?" he asked, trying to sound calm. Deep in the Steve suit, Lola was freaking out!

One of the players from the opposite team turned to Chase and Logan. "Come on, you guys gonna play or forfeit?" he asked.

Logan glared openly at Steve. He was not about

to forfeit, but that meant Steve needed to get in the pool. now. What was the dude's problem?

nicole and Zoey raced up to the pool, carefully avoiding Chase and Logan's line of sight.

"Where is Quinn?" nicole asked, looking around in a panic. There were a lot of guys in the pool. A lot of cute guys. She quickly checked her outfit — pink capris and a matching pink-and-orange tank top. But she'd gotten ready so quickly, she didn't even have time to do her hair! Was it frizzing?

"I don't know," Zoey admitted, throwing up her hands. "She said she'd be here."

The guys in the pool were getting antsy. "Come on!"

"now!"

"Let's play!"

"We're not forfeiting," Logan reassured his team. He turned to Steve one last time. "Would you just put on your trunks and get in the pool?" he practically begged.

Steve was looking at the water with a pained expression on his face when Quinn quietly approached the pool from the other side. She carried a little bag that was moving ever so slightly. Her eyes twinkling,

Quinn lifted a five-foot orange-and-black striped snake out of the satchel. "Okay, Marvin," she said with a sly grin. "Do your thing!" She tossed the snake into the pool. *Plop!*

It only took five seconds for someone to panic.

"Snaaaakkke!" one of the water basketball players screamed, frantically paddling to get away from the slithery swimmer.

"Snake?" Zoey repeated, scanning the water.

In half a second the entire pool was a splashy, chaotic mess.

"Snake!"

"Help!"

"Get me out of here!"

The lifeguard blew his whistle. "Get out of the water!" he shouted. "Everyone, out of the pool!"

Screaming kids scrambled around and past one another as they tried to make it to the stairs.

A panicked kid ran along the pool deck screaming, "Ahhhhhh!" He was going so fast, he crashed right into Steve, who fell into the water with a tremendous splash.

A second later Lola emerged, her long hair falling over her shoulders and her boy's wig floating away behind her.

Logan stared at the girl in the pool in shock. Steve had gone in. He'd seen it. But what came out was . . . "Lola?"

Chase shook his long dark curls to try and clear his head. "I am so very confused right now," he said, staring at the transformed Steve.

Logan turned to Zoey and Nicole, who stood by the side of the pool looking unusually sheepish.

"Somebody start talking," he demanded.

Lola looked up at them with wide brown eyes. They were totally busted. The show was over and it was time to come clean.

"Well, we wanted to prove to you guys that guys can be guys even with a girl around," Zoey explained.

"And that if girls make you act differently, it's just because you're being idiots," Lola said.

"Yeah, it has nothing to do with biology," Nicole added, pointing an angry finger at Logan.

"Yes it does!" Logan insisted. He wasn't about to let a girl — even a cute one — call him an idiot and get away with it.

"You hung out with Steve for a whole day, and did you act any differently?" Zoey made invisible quotation marks in the air with her fingers when she said the word Steve.

"Noooo," Nicole answered before the guys could get a word in.

"You treated me just like a guy," Lola pointed out. She kind of liked it, actually.

"Wow, you people really want to hang out on our roof, don'tcha?" Chase asked, raising an eyebrow. He had to admit he was impressed with how far the girls would go, and how well they pulled off their scheme.

"No, we wanted to prove a point," Nicole insisted.

"But your roof is pretty nice," Zoey admitted with a smile.

"Yeah, and ours is all icky." Nicole pushed her lower lip out in a pout.

"So . . ." Zoey said.

"So . . ." the other girls echoed.

Logan and Chase sighed. Maybe hanging out with girls on their roof wasn't such a terrible idea after all. . . .

CHAPTER 18

Pox Pox

In the infirmary, Dustin rolled over and snuggled under the covers. Life in the infirmary was really comfy . . . for him, anyway.

Across the room, Michael looked around for any sign of Nurse Krutcher. Thankfully, the coast was clear.

Pushing aside his covers, Michael slipped out of bed. It was time to make his escape. He was through with medical torture.

One slow step at a time, he tiptoed across the room. He was halfway there when he stubbed his pinky toe on the leg of Dustin's bed. Ouch! For such a little appendage, that tiny toe sure could smart!

Dustin opened his eyes. "Hey," he greeted in a whisper. "Where you goin'?"

Michael put a finger to his lips. "*Shhh*. I'm sneakin'

out." Looking over his shoulder one last time, he tiptoed over to the exit. Freedom was only a doorway away!

Unfortunately, Nurse Krutcher pushed the door open at that exact moment, catching them both by surprise.

"Ahhhh!" she screamed.

"Ahhhh!" Michael screamed back. Even without a giant needle in her hand, Nurse Krutcher was scary.

"What's going on?" Nurse Shannon asked, rushing in from the next room.

"Where do you think you're going?" Nurse Krutcher asked, glaring at Michael and planting her hands on her hips.

"I'm leaving, all right?!" Michael shouted. "I'm fine, okay? I'm not sick, I was just faking the whole time. So you tortured me for nothing, all right? Now goodbye!" He started to leave, but Nurse Shannon grabbed his arm.

"You're scratching," she said gently.

"So, I'm itchy," Michael admitted, still determined to make it out the door.

Nurse Krutcher threw his head back to get a good look at his face. "You have the chicken pox," she announced.

"What?" Michael couldn't believe it.

"You must have caught them from Dustin," Nurse Shannon said sadly.

Dustin looked at Michael sheepishly. "I'm sorry," he whispered.

Michael couldn't believe it. "I got the pox?" he said, shocked. Then he straightened. "I don't care. I'm leaving. I am not staying in this house of hurt." There was no way, no how . . .

"Lay down," Nurse Krutcher ordered.

"I am —"

"LAY DOWN!" she yelled at the top of her lungs.

"Ahhhh!" Michael fell to the floor, then crawled like a baby back to his prisonlike bed.

The guys' roof was hopping. Practically the whole gang was there.

"I cannot believe I have two book reports due on Monday," Zoey griped as she soaked up some sun.

"Well, I have the same two book reports due, and a chemistry test," Chase one-upped her as he took a sip of soda and flipped through a skater magazine.

"Well, I have to give a half-hour oral report." Nicole topped them both. Oral reports were the worst.

Zoey took a sip of her Blix. "Hey, pass the suntan lotion, would ya?" she asked.

Chase handed over the bottle. "Lotion," he said.

Lola adjusted her sunglasses and sat back with a smile. So far, hanging out on the guys' roof was going great — there was no weirdness. "Ya see?" she said. "Guys, girls hanging out. And no problems."

Beside her, Logan grabbed a handful of popcorn out of a bowl. "Yeah, we'll see," he said skeptically. After all, it was only a matter of time.

Nicole reached over and snatched a few of Logan's buttery kernels. "Hey," she said, looking around while she munched. "Where's Quinn?"

Zoey eyed the crowd. "Oh, yeah, what happened to Quinn?"

On the other side of campus, Quinn sat on a floating lounge chair in the pool. She was holding Marvin the snake and gazing into his beady little eyes.

"Oh, Marvin," she cooed. "You make me laugh." She had never seen such a small creature cause such a big stir. It was amazing!

The snake flicked out his tongue at her, smelling the air, while Quinn's girly giggles echoed in the Pacific sunshine.